The Roya
Witch c

Sarah Shafi

Illustrated by Tony Husband

More Ridiculous Witches by Sarah Shafi
available now...

The Blurting Blabbermouth Witch of York

The Ludicrous Pie-Eating Witch of Wigan

Coming soon...

The Footie Mad Minging Witch of Manchester

The Odd Legged Car Crashing Witch of Leeds

The Flaming Blazing Witch of London

www.ridiculouswitches.com

First published in paperback by Hocus Pocus Publishing in Great Britain
Printed and bound in England by Wheelden Print

ISBN: 978-0-9927193-0-2

British Library Cataloguing in Publication Data available.

For my darling Persia

...and all the children at St Chad's Primary School

With love and thanks to my brother Saleem for his infectious enthusiasm from the very beginning, to Caroline Roberts-Cherry for giving me the nod and being there from the start, to Sarah and Elizabeth Stewart who heard it first over breakfast, to Catalina, Sedona, Yvonne and Brett for being my first amazing family audience, to Shamsi Pearson for being a top notch grown-up reader and champion, to my agony aunt Jane London (and of course Emma, Amy, Joe & Garth), who were always there with coffee and cake, to my ex-hubby Russ for nattering me to get on with it, to Elspeth Taylor for her sensational editing talent, and to Shelley & Janet who giggled uncontrollably and made me feel great.

1

Hold on

PPPFFFFFFAAARTT!!!

...And with that, her long black skirt blew up in the air.

After nearly jumping out of her skin, the lady in the long black skirt looked over her shoulder and shrieked, in a horribly high pitched but a bit posh voice...

"WHOOO did THAAAT".

There was nobody there.

Well, nobody except the lady in the long black skirt. She was quite alone. But the lady in the long black skirt was no ordinary lady.

She was a strange sort of character and her face looked rather odd. It was round and friendly enough but her lips were thin, shrivelled and almost black. She had lovely long eyelashes but then had a great big horrible hairy wart under her left eye.

She looked most peculiar.

That's because she was in fact the Royal Trumping Witch of Windsor.

Royal?

Well, the truth is, she's not Royal at all. She just thinks she's Royal because she lives in Windsor, which (if you didn't know) is very famous for having a rather fancy castle where people speak terribly posh and the Royal family and Queen Elizabeth herself live.

In fact she is so convinced she is Royal, she's made herself a wobbly crown out of tin foil and old scraps of wire that keeps slipping down to one side of her head. She's even stuck shrivelled up red berries on it with superglue to make them look like Royal rubies.

Everyone can tell it's not a real crown though, but The Royal Trumping Witch of Windsor will have none of it. She actually claims to be the long lost Great Grand-Niece of Queen Victoria and insists her crown came directly from The Tower of London, where it was stored for about one hundred years, before she stole it back one night with a bit of string and a coat hanger (but that's another story).

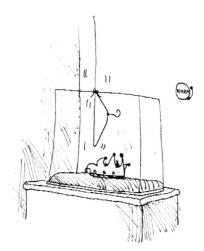

Now, The Royal Trumping Witch of Windsor, who everybody has nick-named 'Witchy Trumps', even claims to have Royal blood. But, like the Ridiculous Witch she is, she has no idea that Royal blood is blue and her blood, like every other witches' blood, is black.

I guess you're probably wondering why she is called the Trumping Witch.

Well, Witchy Trumps has got a problem down below.

It's a serious problem.

When she was a little witch she somehow managed to swallow a balloon. From then on, every time Witchy Trumps opened her mouth to talk, or even breathe, the balloon inside her tummy would fill up with air.

As the balloon inside her tummy got bigger and bigger, the top bit (where you tie it) simply pressed against the inside of her tummy and so the balloon would close all by itself.

But, as the food travelled out of her tummy and down the pipes to make that smelly stuff that plops out of your bottom, it made a bit of extra room inside her tummy and as quick as a flash the top bit of the

balloon would open up again and suddenly, very quickly the balloon would deflate.

You know, just like when you blow up a balloon and suddenly let go of it, it flies around the room making the loudest farting sound.

That's exactly what happened inside Witchy Trumps tummy. She would let out this rip roaring ferocious trump that could blow holes in her pants.

She has even been known to blow little children and dear old ladies right off their feet.

But would she have it. Oh no. Not Witchy Trumps. She didn't believe it was ever her who kept blowing those trumps.

Nope.

Not for one minute.

She would always blame it on anyone who was near her and get absolutely furious with them.

Now let me explain why poor old Witchy Trumps kept blaming everybody else when she trumped.

It's because she could not feel a thing when she let one off!

She has trumped so much and so ferociously since she was a little witch that her bottom has gone completely numb with all those years of trumping.

She didn't even believe it was her who had been blowing holes in her pants.

Why not?

Well it's because she thought her pants were being eaten by moths.

Moths?

You see there were always a moth flying about her house ever since she blew a crack in her chimney a few years back, (which Witchy Trumps thought had been caused by the wind outside, *not* the wind from her bottom).

But this moth didn't seem particularly affected by her explosive trumps though, probably because it was already up in the air flying about anyway.

Now this moth was a very unusual moth. In fact not many people had even heard of this type of moth.

That's because it was a Cremda Moth.

Cremda Moth?

Yes and it was bright green and smelled of mints.

Mints?

You see, Cremda Moth was a very special moth.

It didn't come from around here.

It came from Witches Land.

But why did it smell of mints?

Well, Cremda Moth's have magic
mint making power. They squirt
out trails of green mint sap and
when you collect it and roll it up
between your fingers, into whatever
size you like, it turns into Green
Mint Gum.

And Green Mint Gum is a
witches' favourite thing to chew on.

If you've ever come across a
witch (it might shock you to know
there's usually at least one in every

city), you'll probably notice them chewing something.

It'll most likely be Green Mint Gum.

It hides their bad breath.

You see, most witches have horrible smelly breath (except for Good Witches of course). It stinks like toilet drains.

Luckily for the Witches in Witches' Land, there are Cremda Moths everywhere.

But why had Cremda Moth come all the way from Witches Land?

Well, Cremda Moth was on a mission.

She had come to try and put a stop to Witchy Trumps dreadful trumping behaviour.

You see, even though Witchy Trumps didn't believe (or even know) she's a witch, it didn't stop her from being one did it?

Anyway, I'm sure you'll agree, Witchy Trumps' horrendous trumping and explosive outbursts were totally unacceptable behaviour for any kind of witch. Whether Good Witch or Wicked Witch, Witchy Trumps was not very good

at being a witch at all.

And it was all because she just wouldn't believe that she *was* a witch.

Let's face it, if you are a witch, you might as well get on with it and behave like a witch.

Some of you know there are Good Witches and Wicked Witches. But when you can't get to grips with being a witch, whether it's good or wicked, Witches' Law declares you a Ridiculous Witch. And you must remain a Ridiculous Witch until you sort your problem out once and for all.

And Ridiculous Witches are the worst of all. They are capable of anything...and everything.

They are a complete disaster.

2

Ouch!

It was just before Spring and Witchy Trumps decided it was time to plant some new plants in her garden.

Unlike Wicked Witches, Witchy Trumps really loved flowers (Good Witches often do) but she could never seem to grow any of her own.

The problem was, every time she

tried to grow flowers in her garden, instead of pretty flowers popping up, there would be sharp spikes that grew out at the top of the stems instead.

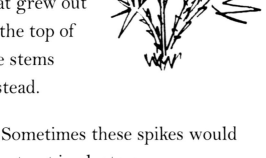

Sometimes these spikes would shoot out in clusters so close together they looked just like tiny broomstick heads.

Imagine how ridiculous that looked.

Now, there was actually a very special reason for this.

Cremda Moth had spoken to all the flowers in the garden and told them under no circumstances were they allowed to produce any flowers. Instead they were ordered to shoot out sharps spikes and thorns instead.

Cremda Moth had put Mr Thorny Bush in charge of the

garden. He was a huge thorny bush that had sharp spikey thorns all over. If he saw even the faintest peep of a flower, he would set his sharp spikes on it and give the poor thing a nasty shock.

And as much as all the flowers wanted to come out and show off their pretty faces, they wouldn't dare, because they knew Witchy trumps needed to learn her lesson. It was for the best, so they did as they were told and longed for Witchy Trumps see that she *was* a witch.

Besides, Mr Thorny Bush was just too terrifying.

But did Witchy Trumps learn her lesson?

Oh No.

Witchy Trumps didn't take any notice at all.

She was so angry because she could never grow any flowers of her own and was always getting pricked by the sharp thorny spikes, so she shouted at the thorns and wished *all* the flowers everywhere in the world would die.

And this is what made Cremda Moth's and Mr Thorny Bush's job a whole lot easier.

You see what Witchy Trumps didn't realise was that when she made a wish it wasn't actually a wish at all...

It was a SPELL!

...And witches spells can only

come true if carried out properly by a real witch.

Ok, so Witchy Trumps was a real witch but because she didn't *believe* she was, her spells would never work on anyone else.

They would only work on *her*.

So, Mr Thorny Bush didn't have to bully the flowers very much at all. Witchy Trumps had doomed them with her own spell.

Anyway, surrendering to a garden full of thorny bushes, Witchy Trumps decided to go the Garden Centre to try and find some new ones.

Of course she was wearing her
crown which she had adorned with
a few more berries for an extra
fancy effect.

After she had trumped her way
to the Garden Centre (blowing over

a couple of rubbish bins and a small dog along the way), Witchy Trumps spotted some thorny bushes just inside the Garden Centre doors which had tiny little orange flowers on them.

She was so excited when she saw them (because it wasn't very often you see thorny bushes with flowers on) that she gasped for breath...

Of course when she gasped, the balloon inside her tummy filled up with air extra quick and then suddenly...

PPPFFFFFFFFFAAAAARTT!!!

It was pandemonium!

Not only did Witchy Trumps blow herself half way across the store, she blew off the entrance door, 6 plant pots and the security guard who was standing nearby.

*"HELP! HELP! "*She cried as she lay flat out on the Garden Centre floor.*"OOOH GOOOOODNESS GRAAACIOUS!*

*I WANT TO SEE THE
MANAGER
IMMEEEEEDIATELY.
HEEEELPP!"*

Her crown had fallen off her
head and had landed on a heap of
smelly compost.

Witchy Trumps was furious.

After helping the security guard
stand up again, the Garden Centre
Manager, Mr Compost marched up
to Witchy Trumps and said *"Now
look Madam"*.

He was very cross but tried to
remain calm, as any good Manager
would.

Before Mr Compost had chance to say anything else, Witchy Trumps, who was by now shaking all the smelly compost off her crown, yelled...

"THOSE TERRRRIBLE DOOOOORS TRIED TO KIIILL MEEE! I SHOULD HAVE YOOOOU ARRRRRESTED I TELL YOOU!"

Mr Compost stood firm and said in his most professional voice...

"Look Madam, I need to ask you to leave this store RIGHT NOW. You MUST get that problem of yours sorted out. I'm

AFRAID WE CANNOT LET YOU INTO OUR STORE EVER AGAIN IF YOU DO NOT. IT IS YOU WHO HAS CAUSED ALL THIS DAMAGE AND IF YOU DON'T LEAVE NOW I SHALL HAVE TO CALL THE POLICE".

"HOWWWW DAAARE YOOOU SAY THAAAAT!" shouted Witchy Trumps. *"DOOOO YOU KNOOOW WHOOO I AAAM"* she had by now secured her crown back on her head.

Of course Mr Compost knew she was Witchy Trumps. She'd been coming into the store for years and every single time she came in she had caused some sort of damage by blowing things over with her terrible trumps.

Witchy Trumps was so outraged that she yelled at him again...

"I WISH THAT AAAAWLL YOUR DOOOORS WOULD FALL OOOWFF AND YOUR WINDOWS WOULD ALL SMAAASH"

Witchy Trumps was really angry and just could not understand why Mr Compost was being so very rude to her yet again.

So she carried on shouting...

"AND WHAT'S MOOORE, I WISH THAT YOOOOU GET A NAAAASTY PRRRICK FROM AAAAWLL YOUR THORNY BUSHES!"

And with that she was off, trumping her way home, muttering under her breath all the while.

3

Yeeoooow!

When Witchy Trumps arrived home she could not believe her eyes.

Her front door was lying on the ground!

It had broken clean off its hinges.

Then as she looked around, she noticed that every single window in her house was smashed.

She peered in through one of her broken windows and to her horror saw that even the doors inside her house had broken off too.

How very, very odd she thought to herself. That was exactly what she had wished to happen at the Garden Centre.

She tried to tidy up as best she could but grew tired and decided to sit in her garden and have a rest.

Mind you, her garden wasn't exactly the place to relax.

It was full of thorny bushes.

But because Witchy Trumps was

so tired she fell into a deep sleep.
Her mouth was gaping wide open,
she was snoring very loudly and she
was taking in lots and lots of air.

Suddenly....

PPFFFFFFFFAAAAAAAAAA
AAAAAARRRRRRTTTTTT!!!!

It was the biggest and loudest
trump of all. Witchy Trumps woke
up with a start.

All around her was total
mayhem. Every single thorn bush
in Witchy Trumps entire garden
was blown clean out of the ground
and about one thousand sharp
spikes were set free and shot

straight up into the air.

But as the thorny spikes made their way back down to the ground, Mr Thorny Bush (who was up in the air with them) gave the spikes a very firm command and suddenly all the spikes turned together and pointed in one direction...

They were headed straight for Witchy Trumps!

EEEAAAAAOOOOOOOOOWW WWW!!

Screamed Witchy Trumps, as one thousand sharp spikes stuck hard into her bottom. It gave her the biggest nastiest shock of her life and with that she flew straight up in air.

She landed with a crash and then promptly fainted.

Now what happened next was quite remarkable.

When Witchy Trumps came to

she was in agony. Her bottom was hurting her like mad. It was sore and stinging all over.

Cremda Moth was hovering over her.

Just at that moment something very strange suddenly occurred to Witchy Trumps...

She could actually FEEL her bottom again!

She tried to sit down to settle herself but her bottom was so sore that she leapt off the chair and screamed.

Of course as she screamed, what

did she do?

She opened her mouth and took in some more air.

PPPPFFFFFAAAARRRT!!!

Witchy Trumps chair blew over and she landed face down straight into some mud.

She could not believe she had trumped.

It really hurt.

Only then did Witchy Trumps slowly start to realise that it must have been her who had been trumping and leaving a trail of disaster all along.

She remembered what had happened at the Garden Centre earlier that day and knew that it must have been her who caused all the damage.

Oh dear.

Witchy Trumps was very

embarrassed.

She then thought about everything long and hard.

You see Witchy Trumps had often wondered to herself why it was that everywhere she seemed to go there would always be some sort of disaster and that she would end up being blown about in all sorts of directions.

Then Witchy Trumps thought about what terrible things she had wished to happen at the Garden Centre. Again, she wondered to herself why it was that whenever she wished something nasty would happen to someone else it would always end up happening to her.

"Maybe I AAAAM a witch aaarfter aaawll" she declared.

And she let out a little trump.

"Ouch!"

Now Witchy Trumps could understand *why* everyone called her 'Witchy Trumps'.

She felt very ashamed of herself.

Suddenly Cremda Moth then flew onto Witchy Trumps shoulder and started flapping her beautiful bright green wings, giving off the most delightful mint  fragrance. It was the loveliest smell Witchy Trumps had ever smelled and the prettiest thing she had ever seen.

Cremda Moth then flew over to Mr Thorny Bush, thanked him and told him his job was done.

Faster than the blink of an eye, Mr Thorny Bush disappeared and was never seen again.

4

Mirror Mirror

A day had passed and Witchy Trumps could bear the pain of all that trumping no longer. She decided that it was time to do something about her problem.

So, she went to see Doctor Hocus-Pocus.

He was a Witch Doctor (but looked decidedly like a normal doctor).

She told Doctor Hocus-Pocus everything that had happened and that she felt very sad because she now believed she was nothing but a wicked old trumping witch. She really didn't want to be wicked at all but somehow she just couldn't help it.

So she started sobbing.

...and trumping.

Cremda Moth was still on her shoulder and would not leave her side.

Doctor Hocus-Pocus reassured Witchy Trumps by saying that not all witches were Wicked Witches and the only way to tell a Good Witch from a Wicked Witch was if she had a kind and friendly face. He continued by telling her that it's only when a witch *believes* she's a witch that the *true* witch is revealed.

He had noticed Cremda Moth and knew instantly where she had come from. He then explained that Cremda Moths only ever try to rescue Good Witches.

Doctor Hocus-Pocus declared he thought Witchy Trumps was a Good Witch.

He then held up a mirror to her face.

To her amazement, Witchy Trumps lips were now soft and pink and her horrible hairy wart had disappeared completely!

A big friendly smile grew across her face.

In fact she looked rather pretty.

Dr Hocus-Pocus explained that the reason she kept thinking she was Royal was because she actually *was* Royal.

Well sort of.

You see in Witches Land, Good Witches are also called 'QUEENS', so the Good 'Queen' Witch inside her must have been trying to come out of her somehow.

How on earth she came up with the Queen Victoria story we will never know.

Now that Witchy Trumps *believed* she *was* a real witch, Dr Hocus-Pocus told her that she could actually stop her trumping very easily.

All she needed to do was *wish* that her trumping would stop and never return.

And so she did.

From that very same day, the balloon inside Witchy Trumps tummy must have simply dissolved away because Witchy Trumps never trumped again.

5

Shock!

A few days later Witchy Trumps decided to be a very brave Good Witch and plucked up the courage to go and see Mr Compost at the Garden Centre.

He was quite shocked when he saw her standing in his store again and came storming up to her. But as he got closer he noticed that she looked entirely different.

She wasn't wearing a long black skirt anymore (which she always did). Instead, she had on a frilly pink and purple knee length skirt and wore a neat blue cardigan over the top. Then, when he took a closer look at her, he noticed that the horrible hairy wart, which always used to make him want to pull it right off her face, had gone too.

Mr Compost was in shock...he could hardly recognise Witchy Trumps anymore!

She still had the same old crown on mind you.

He then noticed the pretty bright green moth sitting on her shoulder and there was a nice minty fresh smell in the air. Mr Compost had never seen a more beautiful moth in all his life and the smell made him feel a little light headed and giddy.

Witchy Trumps apologised to Mr Compost for all the damage she had caused over the years and promised it would never happen again.

Mr Compost couldn't believe his ears (or his eyes) but was delighted at the same time. He immediately grabbed a small flowering shrub from the shelf, handed it to her and then took himself off for a sit down and a cup of tea.

When Witchy Trumps got home she carefully planted the pretty shrub in her garden.

And do you know what happened?

It grew the loveliest flowers she had ever seen.

THE END

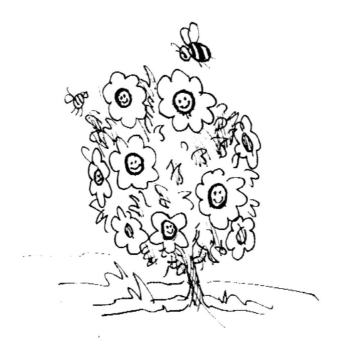